Samuel French Acting Edition

C000241807

The Amateurs

by Jordan Harrison

SAMUELFRENCH.COM   SAMUELFRENCH.CO.UK

FOR PRODUCTION ENQUIRIES

UNITED STATES AND CANADA
Info@SamuelFrench.com
1-866-598-8449

UNITED KINGDOM AND EUROPE
Plays@SamuelFrench.co.uk
020-7255-4302

Each title is subject to availability from Samuel French, depending
upon country of performance. Please be aware that *THE AMATEURS*
may not be licensed by Samuel French in your territory. Professional
and amateur producers should contact the nearest Samuel French
office or licensing partner to verify availability.

MUSIC USE NOTE

Licensees are solely responsible for obtaining formal written permission from copyright owners to use copyrighted music in the performance of this play and are strongly cautioned to do so. If no such permission is obtained by the licensee, then the licensee must use only original music that the licensee owns and controls. Licensees are solely responsible and liable for all music clearances and shall indemnify the copyright owners of the play(s) and their licensing agent, Samuel French, against any costs, expenses, losses and liabilities arising from the use of music by licensees. Please contact the appropriate music licensing authority in your territory for the rights to any incidental music.

IMPORTANT BILLING AND CREDIT REQUIREMENTS

If you have obtained performance rights to this title, please refer to your licensing agreement for important billing and credit requirements.

THE AMATEURS was originally commissioned by South Coast Repertory in California (Marc Masterson, Artistic Director) and written with support from the Goodman Theatre New Stages Festival.

THE AMATEURS was produced by Douglas Aibel, Artistic Director; Sarah Stern, Artistic Director; Suzanne Appel, Managing Director at the Vineyard Theatre in New York, New York on February 8, 2018. The production was directed by Oliver Butler, with sets by David Zinn; costumes by Jessica Pabst; lights by Jen Schriever; original music and sound by Bray Poor; wig, hair, and make-up by Dave Bova and J. Jared Janas; and props master, masks, and puppets by Raphael Mishler. Additional material was written by Heidi Schreck. The production stage manager was Rachel Gross. The cast was as follows:

LARKING	Thomas Jay Ryan
BROM	Kyle Beltran
HOLLIS	Quincy Tyler Bernstine
RONA	Jennifer Kim
GREGORY	Michael Cyril Creighton
THE PHYSIC	Greg Keller

CHARACTERS

LARKING
He plays God,
also Lechery

BROM
He plays Noah,
also Pride

HOLLIS
She plays Noah's Wife,
also Wrath

RONA
She plays Shem and Shem's Wife,
also Gluttony

GREGORY
A set designer
He plays Sloth

THE PHYSIC
Also Henry's Apparition

TIME & SETTING

ACT I: 14th Century Europe
ACT II: The Present
ACT III: 14th Century Europe

In Acts I and III, there might be a wagon, or the suggestion of a wagon – something that can act like a stage but isn't a stage. The special effects for the play-within-the-play should be in line with what fourteenth-century technology could accomplish, with the aid of great effort and ingenuity.

STYLE NOTES

Slashes (/) indicate overlapping dialogue.
The omission of periods in the dialogue indicates rolling momentum.

PRODUCTION NOTES

If an intermission is necessary, it should fall between Acts I and II, with no break between Acts II and III. At the Vineyard Theatre, we performed the play without an intermission and it proved very effective. The Gregory actor had his Jordan Harrison costume underdressed for the final scene of Act I. While the other actors left the stage during the blackout, he simply threw his traveling cloak into the wings and, in what felt like a mere 3 seconds, the lights bumped up on a suddenly contemporary gay man. This may not be right or possible for your production, but I found it extremely satisfying in ours. It helped the audience perceive the monologue as the kind of parenthetical gesture it is.

While this play is written for six actors, there is a seventh role – the surprise role of the Extra Man. In the Vineyard production, our game Assistant Stage Manager played the Extra Man. Or, more precisely: the ASM acted out the part physically, in tandem with a pre-recorded vocal track. It ended up working quite well, though it did take a fair amount of costume and sound trial-and-error to make it come across as sufficiently unearthly.

One of the male actors in the show recorded the lines of the Extra Man, and the sound designer manipulated his voice so that it was very quiet, yet somehow everywhere. The Extra Man barely had to speak above a whisper, as if he was right behind your ear. The dream, of course, is to have a bit of a chill running down our spines, and to end the act with a bang.

If it's financially an option for your theatre to have a seventh cast member, that would obviously be a great – and probably simpler – solution. The most important thing is that we are surprised by the sudden arrival of a seventh player. In other words, the role should not be credited on the cast page.

Are we full or empty at the end of tragedy?
– Bert O. States, *The Pleasure of the Play*

ACT I

Prologue

GOD addresses us. He has a long white beard held in place with string. (GOD is not a very good actor, but he has a powerful voice.)

GOD. I, God, who all the world have wrought,
    Heaven and earth – and all from nought! –
    Now see my people, in deed and thought,
    Are lost in sin so bold:
    Some in Pride, Ire and Envy,
    Covetousness and Gluttony,
    Some in Sloth and Lechery,
    And other ways manifold!

(There is a parade of the SEVEN DEADLY SINS, in crudely arresting masks:)

PRIDE. They call me Pride (of course I'm first) –
    I swell and swell until you burst.

GLUTTONY. Bursting suits me mighty fine,
    For Gluttony is my name:
    My father he was a bacon haunch,
    My mother she was the same.

PRIDE. Look now, here's Wrath:

WRATH. I walk on a bed of knives,
    I sleep with my hands balled up tight,
    From hellfire I was born –
    Return with me to Hell you might!

PRIDE. Now welcome Sloth:

> (**SLOTH** *is the shortest of the* **SEVEN DEADLIES.**
> *He doesn't project his voice enough:*)

SLOTH. I was born on a long slow summer's day
That's already more words than I want to say.

GLUTTONY. Here's Lechery now:

LECHERY. Like Gluttony my cousin,
I live to eat and eat
But Satan knows I savor
A different sort of meat!

ENVY. I am Envy: fear my jealous stare,
For those of you who sit out there
Have took from me my rightful chair!

> (*The* **ENVY** *actor flips his mask, deftly, and
> now plays* **COVETOUSNESS.**)

COVETOUSNESS. And Covetousness, his closest kin:
I'm more inclined to want the chair
Than hate the person sitting in.

THE OTHER SIX DEADLIES. If you have liked us all half-well
We'll see you very soon in Hell!

> (*The* **SEVEN DEADLIES** *start to exit.* **ENVY** *lags
> behind.* **WRATH** *breaks character, but her
> mask is still on:*)

WRATH. Henry?

> (**ENVY** *falls to his knees, dazed.*)

ENVY. My mouth.

WRATH. Henry get up.

ENVY. Tastes like.

WRATH. Get up, they'll know.

> (**GLUTTONY** *breaks character, calling to* **WRATH**
> *from the wings:*)

GLUTTONY. Hollis!

ENVY. My ears are wet.

GLUTTONY. Keep away from him – it's the plague!

WRATH. He's my *brother*, Rona.

> (**GOD** *reappears, on high now. He can tell something is amiss, but the show must go on.*)

GOD. I repent full sore that ever I made man,
By me he sets no store, who am his sovereign.
I will destroy therefore beast, man, and woman,
Who sit in evil's thrall:
Vengeance will I take –
In earth, for sin's sake –
My anger will I wake
Against both great and small!

> (*Lights narrow to a spot on* **WRATH** – *whose real name is* **HOLLIS** – *watching her brother die:*)

HOLLIS. Henry?

ENVY. Tastes like blood. Hears like blood.

Scene One

> (**GREGORY** *speaks out to us, rapidly. His*
> **SLOTH** *mask sits nearby.*)

GREGORY. Two of every kind, he says.

And I say *every* kind?

And he says what are you deaf?

And I say no, Mr. Larking

And he says two of every kind, is that a problem?

And I say well kind of well yeah.

And he says well well well why?

And I say two of every kind is a lot like what about insects?

And he says what *about* insects

And I say well they're so *small* – you won't see all the detail 'less you're

down front. I'll be three days just on the prongies and no one will know.

The prongies? he says

The *(He makes an impatient gesture for antennae.)*, I say.

"*Antennae*," he says.

Like I said, I say.

And Mr. Larking says, Don't you think I do invisible work too? The way I keep my voice warm and my body sharp as a knife? The audience might not know but it makes a difference.

> *(Beat.)*

Plus the elephants, I say

Elephants? he says

And I tell him how it's quite the opposite problem than insects:

If I paint them smaller than a real elephant no one will believe. It'll take 'em right out of the illusion.

And he says Gregory you idiot,

You precious little idiot.

(Which did not put me in a generous spirit)

He says no one west of the Tiber ever laid eyes on a real elephant so how do they know how big?

And I say it's worse then, 'cuz all they know is the *legend*, and legend has to be bigger than real.

And he says you'll figure something out.

And I say I thought I was an idiot.

So I had him there.

>   *(Beat.)*

And Larking says, like he's a new person all of a sudden, he says, "You're not an idiot, Gregory.

At least not when it comes to making things that look like things.

For that, you're the best man I know."

>   *(A proud pause.)*

So I paint us two dogs (start out easy)

Two lambs

Two aardvarks

Two possums

Two by two by two by two

And I stopped before elephants 'cuz I was tired.

And it was good.

>   *(Beat.)*

That's my joke – like the Bible?

"And it was good," like I'm God

Which I'm not.

Mr. Larking is God.

Mr. Larking says he gets to be God 'cuz he's got the best voice.

I'm not allowed to play a part

On account of my looks.

I only get parts where my face is covered.

*(**GREGORY** picks up a lightning bolt he's been whittling.)*

But when it comes to the scenery
And clothes to wear,
And tricking the eye,
I'm Him.
I'm God.

(Continuous into:)

Scene Two

(**LARKING** *enters, still in his* **GOD** *costume.*
GREGORY *whittles.*)

LARKING. What's that supposed to be.

GREGORY. You know. *(Pointing to it like a lightning bolt.)* "Pow."

LARKING. Why isn't it all silver?

GREGORY. Who says lightning's silver.

LARKING. Or gold then.

GREGORY. Where am I gonna find paint like metal?

LARKING. Steal it.

GREGORY. *(?)* Steal for God.

LARKING. From the monks, maybe. They paint pictures on their walls. Must have gold for the halos.

GREGORY. You are low, Larking

LARKING. Says the holy idiot. *(Re:* **GREGORY***'s work.)* How much longer?

GREGORY. All of it?

LARKING. Two of every kind.

GREGORY. A month?

LARKING. You have two weeks.

GREGORY. Two weeks!

LARKING. Then we start performing *Noah's Flood*.

GREGORY. We've never made it all the way through.

LARKING. Exactly. We have to practice or it won't be ready for the Duke.

GREGORY. When they don't like us, they throw things.

LARKING. That's how we get better.

GREGORY. Sometimes it's worse than throw things.

LARKING. How could we know Henry would die on us right there in the prologue?

GREGORY. I have nightmares. The whole town running after us, yelling, Kill 'em all, Send 'em to hell with him!

LARKING. We're actors. They bury us outside the city walls – and that's if they like us. So we've got to be the best they've ever seen, if we want to live.

GREGORY. *(Back to work, shaking his head.)* Two weeks.

LARKING. We'll be ready. I know my lines and the others have less.

> *(RONA comes in, dressed as SHEM'S WIFE.)*

GREGORY. Hi Rona.

RONA. *(To LARKING, ignoring GREGORY.)* Are you hiding?

LARKING. Why would I be hiding?

RONA. 'Cuz you know you deserve a thrashing.

> *(LARKING kisses her neck, but she breaks away.)*

LARKING. What've I done now.

RONA. Saw you looking at her.

LARKING. At who, at Hollis? I wasn't.

RONA. How do you know at Hollis then?

LARKING. I was looking at her like "You should focus on God while He's talking."

RONA. Mm.

LARKING. You know how she goes other places in her head, during a scene?

RONA. I hate her. Always thinking deep thoughts.

LARKING. Her brother died, Rona.

RONA. "Her brother died." And she wanted our best blanket to bury him!

LARKING. Hardly "bury"

RONA. Blankets are for the living.

LARKING. Shhh.

> *(HOLLIS enters now, carrying all the masks in a basket.)*

RONA. Hi Hollis.

HOLLIS. Hi. *(To GREGORY.)* Have you seen Sloth?

GREGORY. Over here.

> (**HOLLIS** *picks up the* **SLOTH** *mask and exits. Immediately:*)

RONA. I hate her.

LARKING. Hate is a strong word.

RONA. I hate you. (**LARKING** *tries to kiss her again. She recoils from his* **GOD** *beard.*) Take that thing off, it reeks.

LARKING. Soon as we get to the river, we'll do a washing.

RONA. You mean I'll do a washing.

> (*For a second, just the sound of* **GREGORY** *sanding his lightning bolt.*)

Can't Hollis take some of his lines?

LARKING. You like lines.

RONA. Ever since he's dead I have to be both Shem *and* Shem's Wife. "Greetings, Husband." (*Turning her head, suddenly in a lower voice:*) "Greetings, Wife." I look insane.

GREGORY. I can say lines.

LARKING. (*Still to* **RONA**.) It's only 'til we find a new Henry.

RONA. Won't be easy. He had the best voice of all of us.

> (*Beat.*)

LARKING. Why are you so cruel.

RONA. If I wasn't, you'd get bored.

> (**BROM** *passes through.*)

BROM. Have you seen Hollis?

RONA. Why?

BROM. I want to show her...

> (*He opens his cupped hands a little: there's a tiny point of light inside.*)

Last firefly of the season.

RONA. Let it go, you fool.

BROM. Why?

RONA. Each one is the soul of an unbaptized infant!

> (**BROM** *looks into his hands, skeptical.*)

They fly around, still looking for God.

BROM. *(Defiant.)* Henry always said they meant hope.

> *(He exits.)*

RONA. And look how that worked out.

LARKING. You're terrible.

RONA. Truthful.

> (**LARKING** *starts to kiss her neck, her hair.*)

GREGORY. *(re: the lightning bolt.)* What about yellow?

> (**RONA** *looks at* **GREGORY**. **LARKING** *still kissing her.*)

Yellow's close to gold.

RONA. *(To* **LARKING**, *whispering.)* He's saying something.

> (**LARKING** *looks at* **GREGORY**.)

GREGORY. We got yellow.

> (**RONA** *snorts.*)

Why don't she like me?

LARKING. Rona? She doesn't like anybody.

RONA. It's true – you all disgust me. *(to* **LARKING**.*)* I know a place we can go.

> *(She leads* **LARKING** *off.* **GREGORY** *pretends to zap them with the lightning bolt, a little half-hearted:)*

GREGORY. Ker-pow.

> *(Then a clap of real thunder, leading into:)*

Scene Three

(**NOAH** *pleads to the heavens.*

BROM, *as* **NOAH**, *wears a fake beard now.*
HOLLIS *and* **RONA** *stand nearby, holding poses as* **NOAH'S WIFE** *and* **SHEM'S WIFE**.)

NOAH. Lord over all, comely King of the sky –
 Noah, thy humble servant, am I!
 Lest that I and my children shall fall,
 Save us from sin and bring us to thy hall
 In heav'n.

   (**GOD** *appears up in the clouds.*)

GOD. Noah my friend, my servant free,
 Righteous thou art, I rightly see!
 A ship soon thou shalt make for thee
 Of tree both dry and light.

 Three hundred cubits, 'twill be long,
 And fifty of breadth, to make it strong;
 Of height? Fifty. And met thou fong; /
 Thus measure it about.

   (**RONA** *holds her pose, but whispers to* **HOLLIS**:)

RONA. "Fong," what's fong.

HOLLIS. (*Sotto voce.*) Rhymes with strong.

NOAH. (*Trying to stay in character.*) Quiet, Wife! God is talking.

HOLLIS. She was talking to me –

GOD. Destroyèd all the world shall be!
 Save thou, thy wife, and thy sons three.

RONA. (*Muttering to* **HOLLIS**, *amused.*) "Three" – I count none.

GOD. (*For* **RONA**'s *benefit, but still in character.*) And all their wives also with thee,
 No matter how shrill and unsavory.

NOAH. Ah, Lord, I thank thee loud and still,
That I, to you, art in such will;
Thy bidding, Lord, I shall fulfill,
On behalf of all mankind.

(He strikes a penitent pose. Beat.)

RONA. *(Muttering.)* Doesn't rhyme with "ill."

LARKING. Rona!

RONA. Seems like it should rhyme, like the others.
Or do you like how it ends all incomplete.
Is that your *thing*, not completing.

(The actors stand there: Are we still talking about the lines? Should we keep going?)

*(**GREGORY** starts to lower lightning bolts from the sky. Creak, creak, creak, creak.)*

LARKING. Not now, Gregory!

Scene Four

*(**HOLLIS** and **RONA** by a stream. **HOLLIS** washes the **NOAH** costume, **RONA** washes the **GOD** costume.)*

RONA. Sounds kind of nice, I think –
  An escape, almost

HOLLIS. Rona, don't say that

RONA. Why not

HOLLIS. 'Cuz it's blasphemous.

RONA. I mean maybe not for forty *days*
  But don't you think all that water? –

HOLLIS. I guess –

RONA. Pure, sky-given water to wash away the rats and the
  sores and the bedpans?

HOLLIS. That whole big boat was a bedpan.

RONA. True.

HOLLIS. I mean, *elephants.*

RONA. Never seen an elephant.

HOLLIS. Me either but you can imagine.

  (Beat.)

  Rona, do you think I'm good?

RONA. As in, not evil?

HOLLIS. Good I mean in the play good?

RONA. You deliver the story of the scriptures to the people.

HOLLIS. But I mean, do you believe I'm *her* when I'm up
  there on the wagon? Do you believe I'm Noah's Wife?

RONA. *(Does not compute.)* But you're not her.

HOLLIS. Never mind.

RONA. You're pretty, if that's what you're / asking

HOLLIS. That's not what / I'm

RONA. In a – untilled field kind of way.

HOLLIS. *(I think?)* Thanks.

(Little beat.)

RONA. I'm sorry about Henry

HOLLIS. *(Taken aback.)* Oh

RONA. I never had a brother, so I don't really know
But you probably loved him?

> *(This is as warm as it gets with* **RONA.** *Something relaxes between them, for a moment.)*

HOLLIS. Can I ask you something?
Are you...?

> *(She looks at* **RONA**'s *stomach.)*

RONA. *No* –

HOLLIS. How do you even know what / I'm asking

RONA. I know what you're asking and no.

HOLLIS. Is it Larking's?

RONA. *(Rapidly.)* No – *(Realizing she's given herself away:)* How did you? – Does it show?

HOLLIS. The way you are with him. You were always so... *(She doesn't say slutty.)* And now the past few weeks you're like the Blessed Virgin.
The Blessed Virgin but with more um anger.

RONA. Do you think he knows?

HOLLIS. I think I know more in my little pinky than Larking does.
Sorry. I know he's / your –

RONA. It's okay. It's not like I'm in love with him.

HOLLIS. But it's his.

RONA. I don't know.

HOLLIS. *Rona.*

> (**RONA** *looks down at her washing.)*

Rona, who?

> *(Continuous into:)*

Scene Five

(Light up on **GREGORY**, *wide-eyed.)*

GREGORY. I'm almost finished painting the grasshoppers and the silverfish and the earwigs and the mites, two by two by two by two, and my arm knew it was working hard when I hear a voice behind me and that voice is a lady and that lady is Rona and she says *Shh Boy Shh Boy Shh.*

And I say if you're looking for Mr. Larking he's not here

And she says *I'm not looking for Mr. Larking*

And I say

Oh.

And she says put your hand on me here.

And I say my hand hurts on account of painting the earwigs

And she says maybe it's better if we don't talk.

> *(A beat, as he takes in the ramifications of this.)*

So we don't.

> *(And immediately back to:)*

Scene Six

> *(Back to the stream.* **HOLLIS** *has stopped her washing.)*

RONA. It was Henry

HOLLIS. You and Henry?

RONA. Your poor dead brother Henry laid with me, it's true.

HOLLIS. *(Genuinely baffled.)* Henry never so much as looked at you.

RONA. All an act.

He was at war with himself. At war with his true feelings.

HOLLIS. Did he know that he – that you were? –

RONA. *(Touching her stomach.)* I've only known three weeks, and he's been gone…

HOLLIS. Twenty-nine days

RONA. Yes exactly

HOLLIS. Your cheeks were dry, when we left him by the road.

RONA. Shock. It was all so overwhelming

HOLLIS. Was it.

RONA. I mean, knowing that I was carrying his seed. Or I mean not *knowing* yet, I didn't *know* – But I think on some level I think I knew I think.

(**HOLLIS** *gives her the side eye.*)

But now, how wonderful: Henry lives on! In me!

And you'll want to help me raise him of course, little Henry.

HOLLIS. *(A touch ironic.)* Or Henrietta.

RONA. I'm not sure that's a pretty name, but yes. And you'll help protect me from harm since I'm the mother of your own dear nephew.

HOLLIS. But I don't understand, what makes you so sure it isn't Larking's?

RONA. The cards told me.

HOLLIS. You and your magic. Those cards don't know everything.

RONA. Actually they do Hollis

Actually that is the *definition* of the cards

That they are tapped into the oldest part of the *universe* and thus that they see everything. *(Beat.)* Also, Larking isn't always able to, you know

HOLLIS. *Oh*

RONA. Well mostly almost never actually.

HOLLIS. All bark and no bite.

> (**RONA** *stifles a giggle.* **HOLLIS** *sees* **LARKING** *coming.*)

Look, here he is now

RONA. Oh no

HOLLIS. That big strapping slice of man-meat

RONA. Hollis don't

HOLLIS. Mr. Bark And No Bite

RONA. Hollis!

LARKING. *(Smarmy.)* Ladies.

You look like you're having fun.

RONA. Here.

> (**RONA** *holds out the* **GOD** *beard. It's sopping wet.*)

Go hang it from a tree.

Scene Seven

(Dark storm clouds signal the arrival of the Flood.)

GOD. The flood is nigh, as well you see;
    Therefore tarry you nought –
    Aboard the vessel you ought!

NOAH. Come Shem, my son, come wife, come all aboard!

*(**RONA** plays **SHEM** and **SHEM'S WIFE**. She does her best, even though she hates it:)*

SHEM. Wife, come with me, if you fear the flood.

SHEM'S WIFE. *(Demure.)* Here I am, husband. Humble wife of Shem, I follow where my husband goes.

*(**NOAH** and his family board the Ark. Only **NOAH'S WIFE** remains behind.)*

*(The animals follow, two by two: A kind of painted canvas scrolls by, showing each species as it is named. If we are alert, we might make out **GREGORY** in the wings, turning the crank that sets the canvas in motion.)*

SHEM. Sir, here are lions, leopards in,
    Horses, mares, oxen, and swine;
    Goats, calves, sheep, and kine
    Here sitten thou may see.

NOAH. Take here cats and dogs too,
    Otter, fox, ermine also;
    Hares hopping gaily can go
    Have grass here for to eat.

NOAH'S WIFE. And there are bears, wolves set,
    Apes, owls, marmoset,
    Weasels, squirrels, and ferret;
    Here they eat their meat.

SHEM'S WIFE. Yet more beasts are in this house:
Each and all from lynx to louse
Here a ratton, here a mouse.

> *(The scrolling canvas stalls. No mouse.)*

Here a mouse.

> *(Still no mouse. Hissing, sotto voce:)*

Here a fucking mouse, Gregory.

> (**GREGORY** *gives the machine a kick. Two mice glide forward, smoothly.*)

SHEM'S WIFE. *(Placid again.)* ...For 'ere they travel together.

NOAH. And here are cocks, kites, crows,
Rooks and ravens, many rows,
Storks and spoonbills, heaven knows,
Each one in his kind.
Wife! Why stands thou there?

> (**NOAH'S WIFE** *turns to him.*)

Why doesn't thou join me on the Ark?

> (**NOAH'S WIFE** *drops character and speaks directly to us, as* **HOLLIS**. *Continuous into:*)

Scene Eight

(Tight spot on **HOLLIS**. *A step outside of time.)*

HOLLIS. Why?

Don't know why.

Never had to know *why*.

I'm only told "Hollis, stand next to the sheep"

Or "Hollis, slaughter the Innocents"

Or "Hollis, birth the Christ child."

Never know why, just do.

If I started asking Why

I'd have to wonder why they welcome us to town by

Dumping bedpans on our heads

And why they say goodbye with tar and feathers;

I'd have to wonder why did poor Henry catch the plague and not Rona

When Rona deserves it so much more;

And why couldn't we bury Henry

Even a foot down even

Instead of throw him on the wormy pile with the rest.

After all that, maybe it's better just to hear

"Hollis, stage left" or

"Hollis, stage right" or

"Hollis, stop breathing through your mouth, you dumb slag, I can't hear my own speech."

There's no Why to worry over.

Still,

It's a lot of time,

Up here,

Time to tell yourself stories.

And now it's stuck in my head, that "Why."

What was *her* Why,

Noah's Wife,

Lady with no name.

HOLLIS. *(Not okay.)* Okay.

LARKING. Great.

(*Silence.* **BROM** *turns the thing on the spit.*)

HOLLIS. Except there's the line / where he –

LARKING. Forget about the fucking line!

RONA. *(Faux innocent; making trouble.)* Forget about the Bible?

LARKING. The line isn't in the Bible, I added the line.

BROM. But you just told her don't put words in / God's mouth.

LARKING. Except for me. The director can put words in God's mouth.

GREGORY. Seems confusing

BROM. Sure does

RONA. Yeah.

(*A beat. Then, suddenly huge:*)

LARKING. MUTINY! MUTINY!

RONA. You're spitting on me.

LARKING. *(To* **HOLLIS.***)* Look what you started, a fucking revolution. This is why they don't let women on stage.

RONA. *(Quoting his own words back to him.)* Her brother *died*, Larking.

LARKING. Two months ago! Are we supposed to crawl into his grave with him? No, we have to practice so that his fucking highness doesn't figure out you're a bunch of talent-free goons.

GREGORY. Shouldn't say "fucking highness."

LARKING. *(Still to* **HOLLIS.***)* Don't you get it? This is our salvation! The Duke's resident players, safe behind his walls. But you know what, if you'd rather join Henry – you can just lie down like him and let the sickness take you. But I prefer to stand up and hitch the wagon and keep on living.

(**HOLLIS** *looks down at her feet. The calm before the storm.*)

HOLLIS. Let the – "Let it take you."

LARKING. I'm just saying that at / some point

HOLLIS. You're saying it's Henry's *fault* he's dead

LARKING. I'm saying there was a point where he stopped fighting, / we all saw

HOLLIS. The point at which he was breathing blood, I think it was.

BROM. Never mind him, Hollis.

HOLLIS. He's saying my brother / deserved it

RONA. Your brother, always your brother. / What about all the others –

HOLLIS. Oh, now he's just my / brother

RONA. It's the same with half of everyone we've ever known. Half of everyone's in the ground now.

BROM. *(Muttering.)* Or not in the ground.

HOLLIS. Exactly: Who's to remember my Henry, on a pyre of everyone we've ever known? In a month, you'll have all forgotten him. And in another year, we'll be forgotten too.

　　　　(Beat.)

GREGORY. *(To the caged doves.)* Coo coo. Coo coo.

LARKING. We'll be in Bergen by noon. There's a square big enough for the wagon and the scaffold. We'll give them *Cain and Abel*, and *The Fall of Man*, and maybe *Before the Fall*

RONA. *Before the Fall* is boring.

HOLLIS. *(Under her breath.)* Paradise – Who can relate.

LARKING. And we'll finish with *Noah's Flood*.

　　　　(A sudden insurgence:)

RONA. What?

BROM. No!

HOLLIS. Every time we've tried it, it's been

BROM. *(Grim.)* Memorable.

LARKING. The Duke needs something new. Something timely. He expects us in December, and already the leaves are turning –

BROM. December, that's three months –

LARKING. *(No time at all.)* Three months to make the greatest thing he's ever seen.

RONA. The greatest thing. I'd settle for another actor.

BROM. Did you ever think of...?

> (**BROM** *looks at* **GREGORY**. *Then they all look at* **GREGORY**.)

GREGORY. Coo coo.

BROM. Never mind.

Scene Ten

*(In different corners of the woods, **RONA**, **BROM**, and **LARKING** all pray to their separate saints.)*

*(**RONA** lays her tarot cards out in front of her.)*

RONA. St. Felicitas, make me a virgin again.

I know I'm asking a lot.

But St. Felicitas,

I believe you have the power to pluck the infant out

And close me up

And make me pure.

BROM. St. Teresa, who defeated her temptations,

Help me forget Henry.

I know God took him back to wash him clean of me,

And so no one will know how we sinned,

But St. Teresa, I still think of him.

St. Teresa, help me find somewhere safe for my thoughts to rest.

Help me not to love a ghost.

LARKING. St. Dominic, help them act well.

Help them be worthy of God's word.

Help them not embarrass me.

I prayed to St. Cosmas last night but St. Dominic, they need *double* the help.

St. Dominic, sit on their shoulders and whisper the lines in their ears when they need you.

RONA. St. Felicitas, make me a virgin

BROM. St. Teresa, make me forget

LARKING. St. Dominic, make them *actors*.

Scene Eleven

(The heavens open. Gold and silver lightning bolts. Maybe **GREGORY** *turns a crank that rolls a barrel with rocks inside, for thunder.* **NOAH'S WIFE** *peers out the window of the Ark.)*

NOAH'S WIFE. The flood comes flowing in full fast,
From every side it gusheth past!
Now all the world is full of flood
O'er every tree we see in sight.

NOAH. This window will I shut anon,
Into the chamber will we be gone,
Till this water, o Mighty One,
Be stopped up by thy might.

> *(***NOAH*** *shuts the window. Two seconds of silence. When he opens the window, the rains have stopped.)*

Now forty days are fully gone!
Send out a dove I will anon.
If earth, tree, or stone
Be dry in any place,
It is a sign, sooth to sain,
That God hath done us grace.

> *(***NOAH*** *releases a real dove. Then* ***GREGORY*** *lowers a lookalike dove, made of wood, from the flies.)*

NOAH'S WIFE. Ah, how fast it returns!

> *(The dove holds an olive branch in its mouth.* ***GREGORY****'s struggling with the ropes – it's heavy.)*

NOAH. Lord, thou hast comforted me today,
For by this sight we may well say
The flood begins to cease.
O gentle dove –

(The dove smashes, spectacularly, to the ground. **GREGORY** *tries to lift it, unsuccessfully.)*

HOLLIS. *(Sotto voce.)* What did you / do!

GREGORY. *(Sotto voce.)* He kept saying make it bigger!

*(***NOAH***, trying to ignore the chaos, solemnly continues his speech.)*

NOAH. O gentle dove, you brought with haste
A sturdy branch from some far place.

*(***HOLLIS*** *is looking frantically for the missing branch. Sweat forming on* ***BROM****'s brow:)*

Hold it aloft, beloved wife
To signal the end of all our strife!

*(***HOLLIS*** *can't find the branch, so she mimes holding it aloft.* ***GREGORY*** *drags the leaden dove off stage, muttering.)*

GREGORY. Bugger bugger bugger bugger bugger bugger bugger...

NOAH. Lord, I thank thee for thy might
Thy bidding shall be done in hight.

*(***LARKING*** *enters in costume. At first we think he's* ***GOD****, but he starts clapping sarcastically.)*

LARKING. Wonderful.

HOLLIS. What're you looking at me for, it was Gregory!

LARKING. *(To* **BROM**.*)* And *you.* If there's no olive branch, you don't stand there like a block of petrified wood in search of its mother forest. You press on, speaking loud and clear!

HOLLIS. *(A brand-new thought.)* Or. What if we were to *acknowledge* what's happening?

LARKING. You mean make it up?

HOLLIS. Rather than pretend it's all going to plan.

BROM. What do you want me to do, improvise in rhyming couplets?

"I see our dove has fallen fast..."

HOLLIS. *(Helpfully.)* "Our troubles surely not have passed."

BROM. Shut up.

Scene Twelve

(Everyone asleep by a dying campfire.)

HENRY'S APPARITION. *(Looking at* **HOLLIS.***)*
> One night, by the fire,
> Hollis dreams she sees her brother in the hissing smoke.

HOLLIS. Henry, is that you?

HENRY'S APPARITION. Miss me, little sister?

HOLLIS. I do. I do miss you.

HENRY'S APPARITION. *(Stark, but not ghostly.)* I come from beyond the river of the dead, with a warning.

HOLLIS. If it's about Rona I already know.

HENRY'S APPARITION. Rona?

HOLLIS. That you laid with her

HENRY'S APPARITION. *(Genuinely confused.)* I never laid with Rona

HOLLIS. I knew it, thank God

HENRY'S APPARITION. And it's a little disappointing that you *believed* her / frankly

HOLLIS. I'm sorry I'm sorry, she's such a tramp. Give me your warning.

HENRY'S APPARITION. I have come all this way to tell you:
> Do not replace me,
> For the man who replaces me will bring you worse than flood.

HOLLIS. We don't have a choice. We aren't just missing Shem – You were Isaac, and the Angel Gabriel, and Mak the Sheep Stealer...

HENRY'S APPARITION. I was versatile.
> But the warning stands:
> Beware the man who would wear my robes and say my lines.

> *(A beat.)*

HOLLIS. In plays, people are always wearing disguises.
How do I know you're my own brother
And not the devil?

HENRY'S APPARITION. My darling sister,

> *(He touches her on the cheek. Scary-soft:)*

The devil has bigger fish to fry.

> *(Lights shift. **HOLLIS** wakes. An unfamiliar man is standing over her, played by the same actor who played **HENRY'S APPARITION**. We'll call him **THE PHYSIC**. It is snowing lightly.)*

PHYSIC. Miss? Hello miss?

HOLLIS. *(Vague with sleep.)* Henry?

PHYSIC. *(Gentle.)* Not Henry.

HOLLIS. Who are you?

PHYSIC. It started snowing – I was passing by.

HOLLIS. *(What next.)* Snow in October.

PHYSIC. I didn't want you and your friends to freeze while you slept.

> *(**HOLLIS** stands, recovering her wits.)*

HOLLIS. The fire's out.

PHYSIC. I'll help you light it.

HOLLIS. *(Almost to herself.)* A conscientious traveler, what next.

PHYSIC. Sorry?

HOLLIS. I will do it, thank you. Now good night.

> *(The **PHYSIC**'s eyes pass over **RONA**.)*

PHYSIC. You have a pregnant woman with you.

HOLLIS. How do you know that? No one knows that.

PHYSIC. I'm a doctor. A physic.

HOLLIS. Never met a physic.

PHYSIC. ...Or I used to be.

HOLLIS. What, you kill too many people?

> *(She was joking, but she sees that it's true.)*

PHYSIC. They want miracles, and that is beyond my training. *(Someone snores nearby, loud.)* Who's that?

HOLLIS. Oh, that's God. *(Seeing the* **PHYSIC***'s face:)* Larking – he's called Larking. But he has a way of staying in character. *(They watch him. Another extra-loud snore.)* He's even louder awake.

PHYSIC. Are you all a family?

HOLLIS. Yes and no. We're players.

PHYSIC. I saw a play once. I didn't care for it. The snake was funny not scary. And when he offered Eve the apple, everyone shouted, "Don't take it! Don't eat it!", but she pretended like she didn't hear us.

HOLLIS. We have lines, we aren't allowed to say just anything.

PHYSIC. The theater is strange. Somehow a hand in a green stocking is a snake, but a real woman isn't a woman – not when she pretends she can't hear us.

HOLLIS. *(After a beat.)* Our snake is better than a stocking. We have a kind of coil that can go long or short, like a real snake.

PHYSIC. *(A touch ironic.)* Magic.

HOLLIS. There's a man who does the effects for us. He has a mind like a child, but he's the best with effects.

(He looks down at **RONA** *again.)*

PHYSIC. Who plays Eve, you or her?

HOLLIS. Rona.

PHYSIC. Of course.

HOLLIS. ?

PHYSIC. *(Re: her pregnancy.)* She tasted the apple and was banished from the garden.

HOLLIS. We're all of us banished. *(Beat.)* You can't hide with us, if that's what you're thinking.

PHYSIC. I'm not hiding. What makes you think I'm hiding?

HOLLIS. You were a physic and now you're not. You haven't slept. *(Off his look.)* Bags under your eyes. You're traveling alone and no one travels alone. And you stop to tell me it's snowing out of the kindness of your heart?

PHYSIC. *(A beat.)*When the baby comes, I can birth it.

HOLLIS. I was midwife to my mother when my sisters came.

PHYSIC. If any of you gets sick, I can / give you –

HOLLIS. Heal us, like you healed the others? You're not magic.

PHYSIC. I'm not sure anyone is magic anymore. Except maybe your man and his retractable snake.

(Beat. Then, suddenly frank.)

HOLLIS. What is happening?

PHYSIC. You mean

HOLLIS. Why is God doing this?

PHYSIC. *(Shrug.)* He's angry with us.

HOLLIS. We've angered him before. But never to the point of...extermination.

PHYSIC. *(Re: the Flood.)* Never?

HOLLIS. Or just the once. And he promised to never again / send the –

PHYSIC. And now He has broken His promise.

(It's hard to tell if that was sympathy or tough love. The PHYSIC stands.)

I am sorry I have nothing to offer you.

(He starts to go.)

HOLLIS. Wait.

Sleep until morning.

(Some darkness and distance between them.)

The birds aren't up yet – you have a little while.
Sleep and I'll tend the fire.

Scene Thirteen

*(The **PHYSIC** takes something from a sack and holds out his hand to **GREGORY**. The others are huddled in another part of the stage.)*

PHYSIC. Know what this is?

GREGORY. Nail.

PHYSIC. Not just.

GREGORY. Rusty nail?

PHYSIC. This nail came from the one true cross.

GREGORY. You mean the cross that Jesus? –

PHYSIC. The very.

GREGORY. Looks too new.

PHYSIC. That's on account of its powers.
  It can heal the sick, if you pray right.

GREGORY. Nah.

PHYSIC. Nah?

GREGORY. Makes no sense.

PHYSIC. Nothing magic makes sense – that's why we call it magic.

GREGORY. I mean: why does it *bring* life if it's what took life from Him?

PHYSIC. Oh, you're a smart guy.

GREGORY. Uh-huh.

PHYSIC. How it works is you drive the nail into a wall or a board, whatever's around.
  And you pray, and it bleeds for the person you want to heal. It bleeds so they don't have to, see?

*(**GREGORY** nods, solemn.)*

Maybe objects do penance, like people. They have to right what they made wrong.

GREGORY. *(After a beat.)* It's a stretch.

PHYSIC. *(Moving to put it back in his pocket.)* Guess you don't want it then.

GREGORY. *(Quickly.)* I do I do.

> *(The* PHYSIC *gives him the nail. He glances over at the others.)*

PHYSIC. What do you think they're talking about?

GREGORY. You.

PHYSIC. Put in a good word for me?

GREGORY. I don't get a vote.

PHYSIC. Think they'll let me stay?

GREGORY. Well, we're short a man. *(The* PHYSIC's *ears prick up.)* I wasn't supposed to say that.

PHYSIC. Out with it.

GREGORY. *(Reluctant.)* There's roles to fill before we get to Travo. That's where His Highness lives.

PHYSIC. His Highness

GREGORY. The Duke who sponsors us. Mr. Larking says if we find favor enough, he'll retain us in court, which means –

PHYSIC. Shelter from the plague.

> **(GREGORY** *nods. Beat.)*

How come they won't let you vote?

GREGORY. *(Matter of fact.)* Because I'm an idiot.

PHYSIC. Says who?

GREGORY. Him.

> **(LARKING** *returns just then, with the others trailing behind.)*

LARKING. Physic!

PHYSIC. *(Standing.)* Yes.

LARKING. Are you a barber as well?

PHYSIC. Only a physic.

> **(LARKING** *exchanges a look with the others. Then back to the* PHYSIC*:)*

LARKING. *(Very rapidly, with impeccable diction.)* Repeat after me: "Six sick hicks nick six slick bricks with picks and sticks."

PHYSIC. "Six sick hicks nick slicks"– I'm sorry.

RONA. Tsk.

BROM. Can you sing?

PHYSIC. A little. What sort of song?

GREGORY. *(Childlike.)* A happy song.

> *(The **PHYSIC** clears his throat. They're all staring. A feeling like this could be a train wreck.)*

PHYSIC. All right then.

> *(But he starts to sing beautifully, in perfect Latin – a pretty, upbeat melody.*)*

VITA BREVIS BREVITER IN BREVI FINIETUR
MORS VENIT VELOCITER QUAE NEMINEM VERETUR
OMNIA MORS PERIMIT
ET NULLI MISERETUR
ET NULLI MISERETUR.

> *(Maybe **GREGORY** joins in with makeshift percussion – a hammer and a plank – helping the song build to a rousing conclusion.)*

LARKING. I'll be buggered. A singing physic.

GREGORY. What do the words mean?

BROM. "Life is short, it will end soon.

Death comes quickly and spares no one."

HOLLIS. *(To the **PHYSIC**.)* That's a happy song?

PHYSIC. It is if you don't know Latin.

LARKING. On behalf of all of us, Doctor, Welcome.

RONA, GREGORY, BROM. *(Generally.)* Welcome. Welcome. Good luck. You'll need it.

LARKING. First you'll learn Shem. There's his robe, and his leather sandals.

---

* A license to produce *The Amateurs* does not include a performance license for any third-party or copyrighted music. Licensees should create an original composition or use music in the public domain. For further information, please see Music Use Note on page 3.

(The PHYSIC regards HOLLIS, who hasn't spoken a word.)

PHYSIC. *(To HOLLIS.)* You lie low, Miss.

HOLLIS. I was outvoted.

PHYSIC. *(Lightly.)* Last night you were my angel. Now you're my chief prosecutor.

HOLLIS. We still don't know your story, Sir. We only know it ended badly.

BROM. *(To the PHYSIC.)* It isn't personal.

HOLLIS. It isn't?

BROM. It's her brother's shoes you're filling. Her brother Henry.

(We see BROM's face, but the others don't:)

She loved him.

(The PHYSIC goes to HOLLIS.)

PHYSIC. We won't forget him.

HOLLIS. I doubt that.

I worry we are built for forgetting.

Scene Fourteen

(In different corners of the woods, RONA,
BROM, and the PHYSIC pray to their separate
saints.)

RONA. St. Felicitas, maybe you didn't hear me before,
When I asked you to make me a virgin again.
Or maybe I was asking too much.
But St. Felicitas, if I must have a child
Then make him a boy, St. Felicitas.
Make him a son.
I don't want a lemon-faced girl.
I want a boy who climbs trees and drives off demons. /
St. Felicitas.

BROM. St. Teresa, make me well.
I couldn't make my thoughts clean
I couldn't stop thinking of him
And the poison has found a home inside me and
feasted there.

> *(BROM takes off his shirt. There are large,*
> *black, egg-sized buboes under his arms: the*
> *plague.)*

Make me whole, St. Teresa.
Not only for myself, but for those who have trusted me.

> *(The PHYSIC makes sure he's alone, then starts*
> *to roll up his long sleeve. There is a little*
> *leather box on his arm, tied in place with a*
> *skein of leather straps. He says the* Birkhat
> Hagomel.)

PHYSIC. Barukh atah Adonai Eloheinu melekh ha'olam…

> *(RONA takes a rose branch and makes a fist*
> *around it. She winces.)*

RONA. St. Felicitas, take this pain and give me a son in
return.

BROM. St. Teresa, take this pain and make me well in return.

> *(He takes out a long metal pin.)*

PHYSIC. ...ha'gomeyl lahayavim tovot, sheg'malani kol tov...

BROM. St. Teresa, take this pain.

> *(Just as* **BROM** *raises the pin to lance a boil, lights shift sharply to:)*
>
> *(***GREGORY**, *driving the Christ nail into the set.)*
>
> *(Bang. Bang. Bang.)*

GREGORY. *(To the nail.)* You be right there 'til I need you.

Scene Fifteen

(Rehearsal. The players ready their masks for the **SEVEN DEADLY SINS** *parade. The* **PHYSIC** *has been given* **HENRY**'s *dual role of* **ENVY** *and* **COVETOUSNESS**.)*

ENVY. I am Envy: Fear my jealous stare,
For those of you who sit out there
Have took from me my rightful chair.

(The **PHYSIC** *removes his* **ENVY** *mask, and flips it over.)*

COVETOUSNESS. And Covetousness, his closest kin –

LARKING. Remember upside down, not just backwards.

PHYSIC. I'm sorry.

LARKING. Don't be sorry. It's the hardest part on account of it's two-in-one.

RONA. *(Under her breath.)* Yeah, whoever had to do that.

PHYSIC. *(For* **HOLLIS**'s *benefit.)* I'm sure Henry was much better.

HOLLIS. You'll be fine.

LARKING. *(To* **PHYSIC**.) The key is find a different voice for Covetousness – maybe he's a higher pitch, *(He says this in a higher pitch.),* so we can tell him from Envy.

PHYSIC. *(Trying a high voice.)* And Covetousness, his closest – *(Bailing:)* I'm sorry.

RONA. I never knew the difference, Envy and Covet.

BROM. Envy is for people, Covet is for things.

RONA. "Thy neighbor's wife"? She's a person not a thing.

LARKING. Not when your neighbor's coveting her.

*(**RONA** rolls her eyes.)*

PHYSIC. How come I play both?

LARKING. We'd look pretty foolish as the Six Deadlies.

RONA. Lucky we don't look foolish.

(She dons her ridiculous **GLUTTONY** *mask, pointedly.)*

LARKING. *(To* **PHYSIC.***)* Even with Gregory we're only six. (**GREGORY** *is nearby as he says this:)* I don't like letting him on stage at all, but at least he's in a mask.

RONA. Maybe he should wear it all the time.

LARKING. Okay you maggots, let's put it all together. From the top.

(The others put their masks on. Even though it's just rehearsal, the room changes a bit – the temperature lowers. As before, a parade of the **SEVEN DEADLY SINS***:)*

PRIDE. They call me Pride – of course I'm first
I swell and swell until you burst.

GLUTTONY. Bursting suits me mighty fine,
For Gluttony is my name:
My father he was a bacon haunch,
My mother she was the same.

PRIDE (BROM). Look now, here's Wrath.

WRATH (HOLLIS). I walk on a bed of knives
I sleep with my fists balled up tight
In hellfire I was born – Return with me to Hell you might!

PRIDE (BROM). And look, now Sloth.

SLOTH (GREGORY). I was born on a long slow summer's day...
That's already more words than I want to say.

GLUTTONY (RONA). Here's Lechery now:

LECHERY (LARKING). Like Gluttony my cousin,
I live to eat and eat
But Satan knows I savor
A different sort of meat!

ENVY (PHYSIC). I am Envy: fear my jealous stare,
For those of you who sit out there
Have took from me my rightful chair!

(The **PHYSIC** *removes his* **ENVY** *mask, readying to switch characters – but suddenly a seventh actor appears, an* **EXTRA MAN**, *already in the mask of* **COVETOUSNESS**. *He wears a black robe and stands very straight.)*

EXTRA MAN. And Covetousness, his closest kin.

(They turn to see him.)

I'm more inclined to want the chair
Than hate the person sitting in.

(An awful little pause.)

*(***BROM** *counts heads:)*

BROM. One two three four five six seven.

LARKING. Seven.

GREGORY. But we're six.

LARKING. Says the genius.

(To **EXTRA MAN.**)

Who's that playing a joke on us?

(No answer.)

RONA. *(A brave face.)* It's the boy who pawed me in the tavern the other night. Isn't it.
What if I give you a dance after all?

EXTRA MAN. You're far too easily had to be coveted.

RONA. Larking, defend me.

LARKING. *(Pretty lame defending.)* If you're looking for a job, friend, we're full up.

EXTRA MAN. No one remembers me?

(The masked figure turns to **HOLLIS.**)

Not even you?

(Beat.)

BROM. *(Very quiet.)* Henry?

HOLLIS. This is an evil prank –
Show your face at once.

EXTRA MAN. Hasty hasty.

> *(The **EXTRA MAN**'s hands slowly rise to his mask. He takes it off: There is nothing underneath but a black void.)*

Now you know me.

> *(**HOLLIS** faints.)*

I took one of you before.
Who will be next?

> *(Beat.)*

BROM. I will.

GREGORY. No!

BROM. The sickness has me already.

LARKING. And you kept it a secret?

BROM. I thought, if I prayed –

LARKING. You idiot, you've killed us all.

BROM. *(To the **EXTRA MAN**.)* Take me and not them.

EXTRA MAN. *(Amused.)* You think I strike deals?

BROM. *(Willful.)* Me and not them.

> *(He holds out his hand to the **EXTRA MAN**:)*

I am ready.

> *(Blackout.)*

ACT II

*(The actor who plays **GREGORY** comes out in contemporary clothes. His manner is very different now.)*

PLAYWRIGHT. Hi. Hello there. I'm the playwright, I wrote this play. And the *[name of theater]* thought it might be a good idea if I talked to you for a little while about, well, *(He gestures to the stage around him.) Why*. It seems that a few ticket holders have been, um, voting with their feet I guess you would say? And I suggested we could just lock all the doors maybe, or like lightly shame people as they're trying to leave, but they said no. No, they said. We are all adults and it would be better if you could maybe just contextualize things a little.

(Beat.)

Now of course I'm not really the playwright – you've seen me already. I'm *[actor's name]*, I play Gregory, but now I'm going to be the playwright for a little while. I've studied him in rehearsal for weeks, studied his nervous tics, his twitches, all his many tics and twitches and I am up to the challenge. *(Re: his clothes.)* This is a faithful reproduction of his drab, post-hipster Brooklyn uniform. He favors plaid. *(Pointing out a spot.)* Ramen stain.

Hopefully you aren't allergic to these sorts of shenanigans – some people are, which is okay. I think *I* even am, a bit. We'll work through it together. *(He looks up at the stage manager's booth:)* The lights are a little... *(The house lights rise a little.)* Thank you. *(To us again:)* That was planned of course. To help this feel

53

like a frank little detour. "Come with me, as we raise the house lights and look one another in the eye."

Because of course, the Vineyard didn't tell me to talk to you. I wanted to. I was writing along, happily enough, and I got to this part of the play, climbed up a mountain it felt like, and – I don't know how else to describe it – I'm not ready to climb down the other side. There are some things we have to figure out first, together.

I'm going to start by telling you about Mr. Shear's 6th-grade Health class and some of the things that happened there. This was, what, 1989? 1990? One of the things I learned in health class was how poorly informed I was, relative to other 12 year olds. I remember one day, my frequent tormentor Damon McCutcheon leaned over and said, "Jordan, do you know what a condom is?" And I didn't know, so I quickly answered, Yes I do, I totally do, and it's *disgusting*. And Damon McCutcheon said, "You don't know what it is, do you." By now a crowd was forming. And I explained, with as much confidence as possible, that a condom is what women wear when they're having their woman times. Everyone jeered, including Mr. Shear, and they lifted Damon McCutcheon up on their shoulders like a hero and carried him off to 5th period.

One day Mr. Shear was given the task of making us terrified of AIDS. He must have done a good job of this, because six years later, when I finally got a boyfriend, I wouldn't do *anything*. No oral, no nothing. We pressed our bodies together uselessly while we kissed, like Pyramus and Thisbe against the wall, only without the wall, and our sweaty torsos made that unfortunate farty sound when they slapped together and apart. Months and months of this, all because Mr. Shear had scared me into thinking if I got a drop of Alex Wolski's virgin cum on my hand I was as good as dead. No, that's glib: The fear was real. It was constant and it was real.

The scariest thing Mr. Shear told us about AIDS was not Kaposi's sarcoma, or the hundred-percent mortality rate, though those were scary. The scariest thing was the story of Gaëtan Dugas, the French-Canadian flight attendant who was believed, at the time, to be Patient Zero. Right away, some things that were questionable to us:

> Male flight attendants,
>
> French-Canadians,
>
> Names with the sound "gay" in them.

Of course, Mr. Shear pronounced it GAY-shun Doo-GAY, not Gaëtan Dugas. Gaytian DuGay had sex with monkeys in the jungles of Africa, then he flew to the jungles of New York City to have sex with *you*, if you let him, and then the next morning he said "Welcome to the world of AIDS" before swishing out of your life forever. Gaytian DuGay, as if daring the twelve-year old boys to send a chorus of "gay, gay, gay, gay" echoing around the classroom. And they did, they dared – and that word stuck in my throat for years.

Later in college, after months of bad sex with Alex Wolski had given way to no sex at all, I was walking through the Castro district with some friends. It's 1997 now. And probably we were seeing *Vertigo* at the beautiful old movie house, or buying a Portishead CD – the sort of quaint, tangible things people did in the '90s. And we passed by a funeral home – I think it was sandwiched between a nightclub and a store for little scraps of Lycra to wear on gay cruises – and I remember saying, Look at that, how funny that there's a funeral home right in the middle of all this, I thought this was like a party neighborhood, how *funny*. And my friend Holmes – who was a lesbian who had been arrested at several protests – my friend Holmes says, What are you talking about Jordan?
What are you *talking* about?

A hundred thousand people died here. The other *day* they died here.

Did you think it was just a place people went to buy little scraps of Lycra to wear on gay cruises?"

Because I was safe in Mr. Shear's health class in 1990, safely learning to be scared, I forgot how people had struggled and fought and died, and were struggling and fighting still. I had never even met anyone with AIDS. Unless you count Mr. Goldsworthy.

Mr. Goldsworthy was a nervous, wholesome man who wore pleated khakis and was probably, no definitely, younger than we thought he was. He and his wife had been childhood sweethearts, eyebrow raise. In his free time, Mr. Goldsworthy coached the debate club and the boys' tennis team. I was on both teams, and a star on neither. The varsity tennis kids did an impression of him that went something like:

> (**MR. GOLDSWORTHY** *appears in a pool of golden light, played by the same actor who played* **BROM**. *He is wholesomely handsome in a sweater vest.*)

MR. GOLDSWORTHY. *(Lisping.)* "Come on boys, let's get nice and sweaty."

PLAYWRIGHT. And an alternate version, which went like:

MR. GOLDSWORTHY. *(Lisping.)* "That's it, boys. Snap those towels."

PLAYWRIGHT. The variations were endless, and always well-received – as long as lots of "S"'s were involved.

Mr. Goldsworthy made us keep daily journals in debate club. And one day, while we were journaling, Mr. Goldsworthy stepped out of the classroom. And my friend Bryan O'Keefe and I – I can't believe we did this – we crept over and read Mr. Goldsworthy's own journal, which was lying open on the desk. We didn't have to look long. At the bottom of the page, in perfect cursive:

MR. GOLDSWORTHY. *(No lisp.)* November 4th, 1993. I can't wait to see Bruce tonight, to explore the city and each other.

*(**MR. GOLDSWORTHY**'s light goes out.)*

PLAYWRIGHT. First of all, "Bruce." Gayest of all names. Then, "Explore the city and each other" – even then I recoiled from the bad poetry of it. But also my heart secretly soared at the thought of this adult escape. If Mr. Goldsworthy could find somewhere, far from the junior varsity tennis team, somewhere truly *(No lisp)* nice and sweaty, then perhaps I could find my way there too someday.

Did Mr. Goldsworthy leave his journal open *hoping* that someone would find it, and out him, and his life would change? If so, we failed him, Bryan O'Keefe and I. We kept his secret, and he stayed in the closet, putting on his pleated khakis every morning. But a few years later, I was home from college and I saw Mr. Goldsworthy at a movie theater. Or someone who looked like Mr. Goldsworthy, only his hair was dyed purple, and he had a tongue piercing, and he looked ten years younger than I remembered. He looked younger than I've ever felt. He seemed barely to remember me, and certainly he no longer needed me to liberate him. He looked young and happy and gay, and six years later he died from AIDS.

(A longer beat. Has he lost his way?)

The question playwrights are always asked is, "Where did the play come from?" And we are annoyed at this question. Probably because we're afraid that the minute we start answering it, we'll be making the whole thing smaller. This is all to say that I didn't sit down to write a play about Mr. Goldsworthy, or the bubonic plague, even. No, for some reason I was interested in a small strange scene from the 14th century morality play *Noah's Flood.*

>   *(The* **BROM** *and* **HOLLIS** *actors enter, costumed as* **NOAH** *and* **NOAH'S WIFE.**)*

Especially the moment when Noah turns to his wife and asks:

NOAH. Wife! Why standst thou there?
Why doesn't thou join me on the ark?
Come in, on God's half! Time it were,
For fear lest that we drown.

PLAYWRIGHT. To which she replies:

NOAH'S WIFE. Yea, sir, set up your sail
And row forth with evil hail,
For without any fail,
I will not out of this town!

PLAYWRIGHT. Yikes. And that's just the beginning, because Noah keeps asking – he begs, he pleads, and still she refuses. Not just refuses – she boxes him on the ears, she spits on him, she curses God. Normally, people in morality plays behave like good little stick figures. They come out and say their name – "I'm Prudence", or "I'm Wrath" – and they are prudent, or they are wrathful, and they get off. Like a school play where the kids play vegetables. But here was this woman who stops the whole narrative cold, acting out a story that can't be found anywhere in the Bible. Driven by a motive that is at best inscrutable and at worst, well –

HOLLIS. Crazy.

PLAYWRIGHT. Thank you. I mean who in their right mind doesn't get on a big boat their husband has been instructed by *God* to build, when the water is rising and everyone without a boat is already floating dead and bloated at your feet?

>   *(**HOLLIS** raises her hand to ask a question, but the **PLAYWRIGHT** doesn't notice.)*

You could argue that Noah's Wife is simply comic relief, of a not-very-feminist sort. After God's long shaming sermons, the players had to make people laugh to keep them from wandering away from the pageant wagon, to keep them from cancelling their medieval subscriptions. And what's funnier than an angry housewife shaking a rolling pin over her head? But I prefer to think of this little passage in *Noah's Flood* as a milestone in the emergence of *character*. An early effort to show a person with real features – with wrinkles, with warts, with a soul. The beginning of "I." Now, why might we be seeing this right at the height of the Bubonic Plague?

> (**BROM** *clears his throat. The* **PLAYWRIGHT** *turns back to the actors, remembering they're still there.*)

Yes! You have an answer!

BROM. Actually I was just wondering if we could –

PLAYWRIGHT. Oh sorry, yes, that's all for now. Thank you both.

BROM. Yup.

> (**BROM** *and* **HOLLIS** *start to exit.*)

PLAYWRIGHT. See you in a few. (*To us, a little sanctimonious:*) You know, I think we can never thank them enough.

BROM. (*Muttering, almost offstage.*) You can thank us by paying us more.

PLAYWRIGHT. What's that?

BROM. Nothing.

> (*And they're gone.*)

PLAYWRIGHT. It's important to mention that, in the Middle Ages, people didn't think of themselves as "I" in the same way we do today. The concept of the individual as we know it hadn't been invented. It took people like Giotto and Tolstoy and Freud and Seuss to form our broad, quilty idea of the self. We'll never know exactly how people thought of themselves back then, but we do know they had no Tumblr pages, no diaries for the most part, no sense that they could climb up out of poverty and own a huge company. Their teacher, if they had one, didn't tell them, "You're *special*, everyone is special." They told them that kings and queens are special and other people are serfs.

What, then, do we know about these noble amateurs making theater in the dark of the 14th century? We know that they were keenly aware of the brevity of life. Every time they said goodbye, it might be *goodbye*. Every play they started writing they might not live to finish. So, what if Noah's Wife wasn't just a cheap ploy to keep the audience from leaving? What if, having watched everyone they knew be tossed on an anonymous heap by the side of the road, they were uniquely compelled to show us a human being as an individual? *(Looking off into the wings.)* Do we have the cards?

> *(No answer.)*

And by we I mean you?

RONA. *(Offstage.)* Coming.

> *(The actors who play **LARKING**, **RONA**, and the **PHYSIC** come out, wearing sandwich boards with paintings on the back. They are slightly ornery about having such a mule-like role in Act II, but the **PLAYWRIGHT** doesn't seem to notice.)*

PLAYWRIGHT. We can see this increasing interest in the individual very clearly in Western painting. First we have a Byzantine Madonna –

> *(**LARKING**'s sandwich board says "Byzantine" on the front. **LARKING** turns upstage, revealing* Crevole Madonna *by Duccio di Buoninsegna.)*

Not without her human qualities, but still less a person than an icon. A tuning fork for our faith. Then, a hundred years later, we have Giotto...

> (**RONA** *turns upstage so that her "Early Renaissance" board revealing* The Virgin and Child *by Giotto di Bondone.*)

See how the eyes are filled with new intelligence, new mystery. (By now, the first lamps of the Renaissance are being lit, even though the plague is still raging across Europe.) Then, a hundred-plus years later, we have:

> (*The* **PHYSIC***, whose board is marked "Late Renaissance," turns around to reveal* The Virgin and Child with St. Anne *by Leonardo da Vinci.*)

...Leonardo and the High Renaissance. The formal pose has melted into a scene of domestic normalcy. Playful, particular – and seemingly painted by someone who's seen an actual *baby* before. Now, Mary is more concerned with her child than with our worship.

What happened here? It wasn't just that painters had grown more adept at perspective, at mixing pigments. They had become more interested in *people* as the main event, not as players in a predetermined divine script. Something had spurred them to think, "Maybe there's no one in charge, maybe we can act for ourselves, maybe we can go off...script."

> (*He notices that the actor who plays* **HOLLIS** *has appeared again in the wings.*)

HOLLIS. Excuse me, *[actor's name]*?

PLAYWRIGHT. I'm sorry, are you speaking to me?

HOLLIS. *(Slight eye roll.)* Sorry, I mean Jordan.

PLAYWRIGHT. Am I running long?

HOLLIS. Well, yes, actually, but I really just wanted to say that I have a story that might be helpful.

PLAYWRIGHT. Helpful?

HOLLIS. I mean, from an actor's perspective.

PLAYWRIGHT. "Helpful."

HOLLIS. ...As you're trying to bring all of these themes together? Coherently?

PLAYWRIGHT. *(Defensive.)* Do you mean the 6th grade health class and AIDS? I'm totally going to tie it back in.

HOLLIS. Totally. But if I could just tell them this thing that happened when I was doing a show –

PLAYWRIGHT. Is this the time you threw up on Trigorin?

HOLLIS. *("And thanks for telling them.")* No.

PLAYWRIGHT. Sorry. Go ahead.

HOLLIS. Yeah?

PLAYWRIGHT. They're all yours.

HOLLIS. Uh. So. *(Really looking at us now:)* Hi. I'm *[actor's name]*. A few years ago now, I was doing a production of *A Christmas Carol* down in Louisville, Kentucky and I was playing Mrs. Cratchit. Mrs. Cratchit doesn't have as much to do as Mr. Cratchit. Bob. I mean there were a few things for me to invest in, like you know I had to pay attention to my kids, to create specific relationships with our many Cratchit children. I think we had eight or nine kids, maybe more – they really wanted to give the local kids a chance on stage – and I had to create you know specific relationships with all of them – figure out who did their homework, who was the bad seed, who liked to torture insects. And of course there was the intense situation with Tiny Tim, who was played by the cutest little five year old girl, she was great. Her name was Hero, which was sort of perfect – she was always keeping me from getting lost backstage. I personally don't enjoy a Tiny Tim who milks me for sympathy and this girl she had a kind of fiery little will, she was kind of spunky and wonderful and, uh. Really played against the disability.

Now, did you know that Mrs. Cratchit doesn't even have a first name?

PLAYWRIGHT. Just like Noah's wife –

HOLLIS. Yes, although in the Jewish tradition, she is called Naamah, and sometimes Emzara.

PLAYWRIGHT. Wow.

HOLLIS. But you knew that, from all the research you did.

PLAYWRIGHT. *(He didn't.)* Totally. From the research, for the play.

HOLLIS. So yeah, originally she didn't have a first name, and the same is true of Mrs. Cratchit. In some of the more feminist-leaning adaptations, people have decided to call her Emily. Thoughtful. But in this version, not only did I not have a name, but the show had been cut down to a sleek intermission-less ninety minutes, and so guess whose scenes had been hacked to pieces? Yes. Mine. And on top of that the director made us all sing Christmas carols during the transitions – just to, you know, make it accessible – so we would all come out in a big group and sing "God Rest Ye Merry Gentlemen" while the turntable was turning, which was problematic for me because I can't sing but also because well, *why*. Why was I singing to the audience and, more importantly, who was doing the singing? Who is the "I"? Is it me, *[actor's name]* (who can't sing) or is it me, Emily Cratchit, and does Emily Cratchit with all of her kids have time to leave the house and sing "God Rest Ye Merry Gentlemen" to...whom? I mean who am I and who is the audience? Who are you? Please don't answer. It's not that kind of play.

So when it came time to sing, I was so paralyzed I couldn't make a sound because I didn't know who I was or why I was there, so I would just: *(She mouths the words to "God Rest You Merry Gentlemen" enthusiastically.)* And then one night while I was doing that, this weird little idea came to me. What if...? What if this whole *Christmas Carol* business, this whole situation where Scrooge gets redeemed, gets taught the true meaning of Christmas by supernatural beings was actually engineered and controlled by... ME. EMILY CRATCHIT. What if this whole thing had been my idea, what if I was the most supernatural being of all, what if I had done some secret spells in my kitchen to raise the ghost of Marley, to raise the ghosts of Past, Present, Future – what if Emily Cratchit was actually a witch, what if I was the *author of this whole experience*? I mean c'mon, who has the strongest motive for getting Ebenezer to reform his ways? Whose idea was this whole thing anyway? Marley's? God's? The Christmas spirits? Boring. I was a real live flesh and blood human woman, nay MOTHER, with eight or nine kids one of whom had a serious disability. I had the motive! My husband needed a fucking raise, and by God I was going to do whatever I could to make that happen. For our family. For my brave little Tiny Tim who never once felt sorry for herself / himself. Even if that meant casting some spells, raising up some ghosts to scare the shit out of my husband's boss.

So this was my "invisible" work. I, *[actor's name]* AKA Emily Cratchit, was going to take control of the narrative from the inside, even if no one knew I was doing it. By God, I was going to have some motherfucking agency. Now I could walk onstage with a sense of purpose! I knew who I was – I was the witch who was in charge of this whole play. I could sing loudly! And if I sang off key it didn't matter because I wasn't trying to sound pretty, I was trying to scare the shit out of you, to get you to take a look at yourselves, to take yourselves on (as my therapist likes to say) before for it was *too late*.

One night before the show I was sitting on the couch sharing a Snickers bar with the Ghost of Christmas Past and I told her my secret. I was afraid she would think I was crazy but instead she said, "Interesting choice." And after that, she always gave me a meaningful look while we were singing "We Wish You a Merry Christmas" at the end of the play, as if to say: "Nice work, Goody Cratchit" and I would nod silently to her, from under my bonnet: "Thank you, Christmas Past, fellow Master of the Black Arts."

I guess my point is that I had to find a way to give myself a sense of purpose and wholeness on stage. I desperately needed a narrative that helped me not feel so powerless. And so, to sum this all up –

PLAYWRIGHT. Yes, good –

HOLLIS. I think this voicelessness – this *namelessness* I had been suffering from, I mean it isn't your brother dying from the Black *Death* maybe, but I think it still relates to the powerlessness we sometimes feel as mortal human creatures. Because let's face it, if you ever stop to think about it, this whole situation, this whole Being a Person, is really just chaos and dissipation and fragmentation, and well basically a death march basically.

　　　(Beat.)

Sorry, that got a little –

PLAYWRIGHT. *(Newly energized.)* No, no! – I mean that was *dark* – but this is good

HOLLIS. Yeah?

PLAYWRIGHT. Because those 14th century players telling the story of Noah's Ark – maybe they were also trying to make their roles a little less nameless, in the hope that they would feel less nameless themselves. And in that effort, the first *characters* were born. From Noah's Wife to *(He looks to* HOLLIS.*)* –

HOLLIS. Namaah –

PLAYWRIGHT. – To Namaah. From Mrs. Cratchit to Emily Cratchit, Secret Witch. From Mr. Goldsworthy to Robert Goldsworthy, secret lover of Bruce.

Yes: it's possible that the reason we're looking at this 14th century epidemic in the first place is because of a different epidemic, and the efforts of some ramen-stained, plaid wearing person to understand the things it extinguished and the things it inspired, and whether he even has the *right* to be inspired by it, having only feared. To understand whether Mr. Goldsworthy left his journal open hoping to be saved. Or did he leave it open to save me, because that's really what he did.

What, then, to take from this little detour? I suspect we can boil it all down to a single (if multi-tiered) question:

Confronted with a crisis, what is the artistic impulse?

Is it to dive headlong in, and record suffering for future generations?

Or is it to make us forget the crisis? To fill us, either by beauty or laughter, with the will to live.

Or or or, is it a rejection of art entirely, a mere fight for survival? A turning away from the luxury of fiction.

And if it's art we choose, then which is art:

An ark to carry us over the waters?

Or a nail that bleeds for us, so that we can be healed?

Yes.

Yes.

Yes.

Yes.

Yes.

> (*He takes us in for a moment, then turns up stage. The nail that he put in the wall earlier, as* **GREGORY,** *has started to bleed.*)

Yes.

> (*Quick fade.*)

ACT III

Scene One

(The **PLAYWRIGHT** *changes back into his* **GREGORY** *costume:)*

GREGORY. Back to the open road.

Back to lice in your hair and no running water and go to bed when the sun goes down. It makes that other century seem fond and faraway.

When last we left them, the players had a visitor –

(Light on the **EXTRA MAN** *entering, as before.)*

And Brom made a sacrifice –

(Light on **BROM** *holding his hand out, as before.)*

And it was all a little much for Hollis –

(Light on **HOLLIS** *fainting, as before. The* **PHYSIC** *rushes to her side.)*

There now, you're all caught up.

And now I surrender my omniscience. (I feel lighter already.) Fourth wall up – You're on your own.

(Light shifts. **GREGORY** *runs to join the others, who are gathered around a hole in the ground.* **LARKING** *is delivering a eulogy of sorts:)*

LARKING. Brom spoke clearly. He remembered his lines. He was the strongest actor, next to me.

(A beat. An amendment:)

He was the strongest actor.

I don't know much else, except that he was from the North and he could mend shoes and he kept to himself. He never complained of the cold.

GREGORY. Probably 'cuz he was from the North.

LARKING. *("Shut up.")* Thank you Gregory.

Brom never spoke of his family, or his loves. He had a job and he did it. I expect to see him in heaven, if I make it there.

> (**LARKING** *throws the first shovelful of dirt. The* **PHYSIC** *and* **HOLLIS** *stand slightly apart from the others:*)

PHYSIC. *(Scoffing.)* Heaven.

HOLLIS. *(Taken aback.)* Do you see him elsewhere?

PHYSIC. My mother told me, "Asher, heaven and hell are the same lie. They're to keep people from living while they've the chance." I was six.

HOLLIS. I'm sorry

PHYSIC. For what

HOLLIS. That you inherited her blasphemy.

> *(Beat.)*

"Asher."

> *(The blood drains from his face. He's revealed himself.)*

It's a Jewish name. And that's why you were running away.

PHYSIC. In my town, they think the Jews are responsible.

HOLLIS. For the plague? They are giving you a lot of credit.

> *(In earnest:)*

I've heard of your people poisoning wells and stealing children, but nothing so...

PHYSIC. Godly?

> *(She nods. A beat.)*

They made a house.

HOLLIS. They / made? –

PHYSIC. A plain wooden house, by the river. It was a house for Jews.

HOLLIS. To live in, separately?

> (*He shakes his head.*)

PHYSIC. There were no windows, which should have been sign enough. All the Jews of the town were made to go inside. Then they lit the torches. Everyone stood across the river and watched it burn. They wanted to make sure the Jews didn't change shape and escape.

HOLLIS. But then how did you? –

PHYSIC. I've kept it secret, for years. Jewish doctors can't treat Christian patients. (**HOLLIS** *nods: of course.*) So it was easy to escape. I simply had to stand there on the bank and...watch.

HOLLIS. Then you weren't running from the townspeople when we met you.

PHYSIC. No. I was simply running. Probably I will always be running.

> (*Beat.* **HOLLIS** *glances toward the others at* **BROM***'s grave.*)

HOLLIS. Did we dream it?

PHYSIC. Six people don't have the same dream. And that's Brom down in that hole, in any case.

HOLLIS. I don't believe that's him down there.

PHYSIC. "Heaven."

LARKING. (*To the unseen others.*) Hitch up the wagon.

> (**LARKING** *comes from the grave now, wiping the dirt from his hands.*)

PHYSIC. Please – keep my secret.

HOLLIS. Why should I?

PHYSIC. Please.

> (**LARKING** *is there.*)

LARKING. We can still make it by the solstice if we hurry.

HOLLIS. *("We're not still going?")* It is mountains away. It is *countries* away.

LARKING. *(As he exits.)* Then you'd better start walking.

Scene Two

*(The **DUKE**'s palace. **LARKING**, **RONA**, **HOLLIS**, **GREGORY**, and the **PHYSIC** are met by the **DUKE**'s officious **MAJOR-DOMO**, played by the actor who played **BROM**. They are freezing.)*

MAJOR-DOMO. You are the players?

LARKING. *(Bowing.)* We are.

GREGORY. Are you the Duke?

LARKING. Gregory –

MAJOR-DOMO. I am the Duke's Major-Domo, I oversee the operations of the palace.
We are full up for the holidays, but there's two cots in there for you to fight over, and hay for the rest. If you want to wash there's a pump by the stables.

LARKING. And firewood?

MAJOR-DOMO. There's woods all around, aren't there?

*(**LARKING** is chastened – a new look for him.)*

Two Tuesdays next is the night before Epiphany, that's when you'll perform for his excellency. He's expecting something more memorable than last year.

LARKING. What was wrong with last year?

MAJOR-DOMO. *(Deadpan.)* He doesn't remember.

RONA. Oh –

*(**RONA** has a sudden dizzy spell. **LARKING** steadies her.)*

MAJOR-DOMO. What's the matter with her.

HOLLIS. She hasn't had much to eat today.

MAJOR-DOMO. Could've fooled me. Fat cow.

*(**HOLLIS** and the **PHYSIC** lock eyes.)*

GREGORY. She's not, she's beautiful.

MAJOR-DOMO. Eye of the beholder, they say.

LARKING. Excuse me, but when do we get an audience with the Duke?

MAJOR-DOMO. An audience with the Duke?

LARKING. For the sake of preparation.

MAJOR-DOMO. *(Preposterous.)* An audience with the Duke!

LARKING. ...So that we may pay our respects, take any requests his excellency may have –

MAJOR-DOMO. No one sees the Duke except his doctor, his chamber boy, his scribe, and his food taster. Even his wife and daughters are on quarantine. The littlest took ill one morning and she was in the ground by sundown.

HOLLIS. How will he see the performance?

MAJOR-DOMO. There is a loose brick in his bedchamber for spying on visitors of state. He will remove the brick and watch your performance, as a prisoner watches the sky through a slit in his cell.

HOLLIS. It doesn't sound very *festive*.

MAJOR-DOMO. If the Duke favors you, he will give you a message through me. That is your audience with him.

GREGORY. Do you have paint?

MAJOR-DOMO. Excuse me?

GREGORY. White paint is best, but orange could also be good.

LARKING. Gregory, you idiot –

MAJOR-DOMO. *(Happy to contradict* **LARKING**.*)* We'll see about some paint for the gentleman. *(As he exits:)* The Duke does enjoy spectacle.

> (**LARKING** *turns to* **GREGORY** *with contempt.*)

LARKING. Paint?

GREGORY. It's for an idea – How Rona could play the other two sons, not just Shem.

RONA. Oh good, more lines.

HOLLIS. *(A beat.)* I think it's colder in here than outside.

PHYSIC. I'll get the firewood.

HOLLIS. I can help.

LARKING. We'll draw straws for the cots.

HOLLIS. Let's give Rona one.

LARKING. Why should she have it, just like that?

> (**RONA** *gives* **HOLLIS** *a look that says, "Don't give me away."*)

RONA. *(Throwing* **HOLLIS** *a look.)* Straw's good enough for me.

Scene Three

>(*Dress rehearsal. Dark clouds signal the arrival of the flood.*)

GOD. The flood is nigh, as well you see;
>Therefore tarry you nought –
>Aboard the vessel you ought!

>(**LARKING** *steps out of the scene and watches from the wings. Maybe he mouths the words from time to time. The* **PHYSIC** *has taken over the role of* **NOAH**.)

NOAH. Come Shem, my son, come wife, come all aboard!

SHEM. Wife, come with me, if you fear flood.

SHEM'S WIFE. Here I am, husband. Humble wife of Shem, I follow where my husband goes.

NOAH. Shem, gather your brothers, younger and youngest.

SHEM. Brothers, come hither!

>(**SHEM** *pulls a cord on his costume that releases his two "brothers," wooden cutouts of* **HAM** *and* **JAPHET**, *that fall to either side of his shoulders.* **RONA** *throws her voice, acting as the other brothers. Somehow she has four roles now.*)

HAM. Here I am Father, your second son Ham.

JAPHET. And I, your third son Japhet.

HAM. Shall we aboard as well?

JAPHET. (*A kind of echo – she pretends to do both voices at once.*) ...As well?

NOAH. Quickly, my sons.

RONA. This is... / awful.

LARKING. Don't stop. Now counter, so that Hollis can move into place.

>(**RONA** *and the* **PHYSIC** *counter.* **HOLLIS** *moves into place as* **NOAH'S WIFE**.)

And Noah says,

NOAH. Wife!

> (**RONA** *touches her stomach.*)

Why stands thou there?

RONA. Oh no.

> (*Her water has broken.*)

HOLLIS. It's not –

RONA. Yes, I think –

LARKING. What now?

RONA. *(To* **HOLLIS.***)* It's coming.

LARKING. What's coming?

> (*They don't say anything.*)

What?

> (*Blackout.*)

Scene Four

> *(Lights up abruptly. The* **PHYSIC** *is delivering* **RONA***'s baby. It is not going well. The others assist, as well as they can.* **GREGORY** *is secretly a nervous father.)*

PHYSIC. Apply the sard stone!

GREGORY. Apply the sard stone!

LARKING. I'm not deaf!

PHYSIC. Hurry.

LARKING. Where?

GREGORY. In your hand!

LARKING. *("You idiot.")* ...Do I *put* it?

PHYSIC. Her inner thighs.

> *(***RONA*** screams, wracked with a painful spasm.* **LARKING** *rubs the large, blood-red stone on her thighs.)*

"Oh happy stone, work your magic."

LARKING. Like this?

PHYSIC. No – closer to, you know

LARKING. What?

RONA. My cunt, you idiot.

LARKING. This is weird.

HOLLIS. Here, I can –

> *(***HOLLIS*** takes the stone and places it between her legs.)*

PHYSIC. "Open up, you dark gates,
  Just as the gates of Hell opened
  For Christ the redeemer and all the harrowed souls!"

> *(***RONA*** screams.)*

LARKING. I can't look.

HOLLIS. It's normal, this is normal.

PHYSIC. "Just as those hellish doors opened,

open now, so that the child may come out intact, and that this mother's life be saved also."

LARKING. Is it working?

PHYSIC. It isn't *instant*!

> (**RONA** *grunts something indecipherable but angry.*)

What'd she say?

HOLLIS. "Men are worthless," I think

PHYSIC. *(To* **RONA.***)* Don't worry, I've done this before.

RONA. *(Through clenched teeth.)* Coulda fool may –

HOLLIS. *(Translating.)* "Coulda fooled me."

PHYSIC. I got it.

RONA. Hollis

PHYSIC. Keep pushing.

RONA. Where's Hollis / I want Hollis

HOLLIS. I'm here, Rona, I'm right / here

PHYSIC. Keep pushing, it's past ready

GREGORY. *(Nervous dad.)* "Past ready," what's that

PHYSIC. It has to come out –
You can see the top of its head there?

LARKING. *("Ew.")* Oh yeah

GREGORY. Has to come out or what?

PHYSIC. It's just – time.

> (**HOLLIS** *clocks that he's being evasive – she knows enough about childbirth to be scared.*)

RONA. *(Exhausted.)* How long have I been doing this now? It feels like all my life.

LARKING. It was dark when you started and now it's getting dark again.

HOLLIS. Rona push.

RONA. I'm so tired

PHYSIC. Rona you / have to

GREGORY. Rona push

RONA. *(Through her teeth.)* Fuck!

PHYSIC. Rona, you're a tough crazy lady, / I know you can // do this for me. Do it for your baby, /// I know you want to give your baby a chance don't give him back to God just yet, take him for yourself first! Hold him in your arms!

RONA. *(Overlapping at "/".)* Fuck!

Fuck.

Fuck.

Fuck.

FUCK YOU, LARKING.

FUCK. YOU.

FUCK. YOU.

HOLLIS. *(Soothingly, overlapping at "//".)* I can see him, Rona. You're so close. You're so close. I can see him.

GREGORY. *(Overlapping at "///".)* Rona Rona Rona Rona Rona Rona Rona Rona Rona Rona Rona Rona Rona Rona Rona Rona Rona Rona Rona Rona Rona Rona Rona.

LARKING. *(Overlapping at "///".)* Rona you stupid mule don't fuck this up for me –

God put you on this earth to do one thing and it sure isn't acting. I want a son Rona, give me a son Rona //// give me my son ///// give me my son

PHYSIC. *(Overlapping at "////".)* Push Rona push Rona, push!

RONA. *(Overlapping at "/////".)* FUCK YOU LARKING IT ISN'T YOURS.

(The baby comes.)

LARKING. What?

*(The **PHYSIC** holds up the baby.)*

PHYSIC. It's a girl, Rona! It's a girl!

*(**RONA** doesn't say anything.)*

Rona?

(No answer.)

HOLLIS. She wanted a boy.

LARKING. "It isn't yours."

(*To* **RONA**.) Whose is it then?

HOLLIS. It isn't crying.

LARKING. (*To* **RONA**.) Answer me, you stupid whore. Was it Brom?

HOLLIS. (*To* **PHYSIC**.) Why isn't she crying?

PHYSIC. She's too early, / I was afraid of this.

LARKING. (*To* **RONA**.) Was it Henry?

GREGORY. (*To* **PHYSIC**.) What's wrong what's wrong?

HOLLIS. The poor little –. Oh, Rona.

LARKING. What.

> (**LARKING** *looks at the motionless baby in the* **PHYSIC***'s arms. They watch, silently, as the* **PHYSIC** *wraps it in a cloth.*)

GREGORY. Can I hold her?

Scene Five

(**LARKING** *and the* **PHYSIC** *are in costume.* **HOLLIS** *sits, only half-in her* **NOAH'S WIFE** *costume. She looks like she's been through a storm.*)

(*The* **MAJOR-DOMO** *stands at the door.*)

MAJOR-DOMO. The Duke is waiting.

LARKING. Yes we know.

MAJOR-DOMO. The Duke never waits.

LARKING. (*Re:* **HOLLIS**.) She's almost ready.

(**HOLLIS** *doesn't move or respond. Not altogether there.*)

MAJOR-DOMO. She doesn't look ready.

LARKING. (*Sotto.*) Put on your shoes, you stupid slag. Don't make me beg.

HOLLIS. (*Not looking at him, biting her words.*) Rona lies in the next room, nearly dead.

LARKING. And you think your stubbornness will make her well?

PHYSIC. Even if we push her out of our minds, who will play her part?

LARKING. I will

PHYSIC. You?

LARKING. If the rest of you speak slowly, and add a few long pauses, I can climb down the scaffold, and tear off the God beard, and get into Shem's costume, while throwing my voice onto the stage –

PHYSIC. (*Dry.*) Who needs the rest of us? You may as well play all the parts.

LARKING. (*Not realizing he was being dry.*) You don't know how long I've considered it.

MAJOR-DOMO. Your answer, sirs.

PHYSIC. (*To* **LARKING**.) Face it, there's no one

GREGORY. There's me.

> *(The three men look at him.)*

I know the lines. I watch every night.

PHYSIC. He knows the lines. He watches every night.

> *(**LARKING** turns away, disgusted.)*

LARKING. Better not to go on at all.

> *(The **MAJOR-DOMO** starts to go. With a trace of sadistic delight:)*

MAJOR-DOMO. I will give His Highness the bad news.

HOLLIS. Stop.

> *(He stops, hearing the authority in her voice. For the first time in the scene, it's like she's completely there, woken from her spell.)*

*(To **LARKING**, a command.)* We will perform. And Gregory will take her part. And we will be saved.

> *(**LARKING** takes in **GREGORY** one more time. Capitulating:)*

LARKING. It will be a night to remember.

Scene Six

(The performance for the **DUKE**. *We are in the middle of the scene where the animals file onto the Ark.* **GREGORY** *stands in for* **RONA**, *playing* **SHEM** *and* **SHEM'S WIFE**.*)*

NOAH. Here are cocks, kites, crows,
Rooks and ravens, many rows,
Storks and spoonbills, heaven knows,
Each one in his kind.

SHEM. And here are doves, digs, drakes,
Redshanks running through the lakes...

*(**HOLLIS** whispers to the **PHYSIC**, as **SHEM** continues to narrate the parade of animals:)*

HOLLIS. *(Sotto voce.)* It isn't going well.

PHYSIC. *(Sotto voce.)* At least he knows the words.

SHEM. *(Continuous, underneath.)*
...Each fowl that to safety makes
In this ship men may find.

HOLLIS. *(Sotto voce.)* I don't mean Gregory. The crowd is sitting on their hands. They're city people – they've seen effects before.

PHYSIC. *(Sotto voce.)* What can we do? We have lines.

SHEM. Camels, donkeys trail behind
Buck and doe, hart and hind
Beasts of every type and kind
Have boarded, thinketh me.

NOAH. Wife! Why stands thou there?
Come in, on God's half!
Time it were,
For fear lest that we drown.

NOAH'S WIFE. Yea, sir, I will not.

*(Beat. The **PHYSIC** is flummoxed, but he stays in character.)*

NOAH. Thou will... "not"?

> (**LARKING** *hisses from the wings, sotto voce:*)

LARKING. You will! She will!

NOAH'S WIFE. Yea, I will not.

NOAH. *(Privately; to* **HOLLIS**, *not the audience.)* Why not?

> *(She kisses him softly on the mouth.)*

HOLLIS. I don't feel like it.

> *(Shifting to* **NOAH'S WIFE** *again.)*

Husband dear, set up your sail
And row forth with evil hail,
For without any fail,
I will not out of this town!

NOAH. Headstrong wife, the waters rise
There is no room for... *(Reaching for a rhyme.)*

NOAH'S WIFE. – Compromise?
Nevertheless it's too unwise
To leave our friends behind.

NOAH. Fine friends to you they'll surely be
If you, with they, are under the sea.

NOAH'S WIFE. Then row forth, Noah, get thee gone
If you're so deft at moving on –
Cut old ties, forget old friends
Dispense with *all*, if it your spiteful God offends!

> *(Maybe there are murmurs and snorts from
> the unseen crowd.* **LARKING** *furiously signals
> to* **GREGORY** *to intervene.)*

LARKING. Gregory!

SHEM. Father, I shall fetch her in, I trow,
Without any fail!

NOAH. Good lad –

SHEM. Mother, look and see the wind,
For we are set to sail.

NOAH'S WIFE. Son, go again to him and say
    I will not come therein today.

SHEM. Brothers, help me fetch her in!

> (**SHEM** *pulls the cord that releases the wooden cutouts of* **HAM** *and* **JAPHET**.)

NOAH. Yes, good sons, make haste –
    Which of you can help?

SHEM. I, Shem, the tallest!

HAM. And I, Ham, the strongest!

JAPHET. And I, Japhet, the...longest-naméd!

SHEM. We all shall help

HAM. *(Echo.)* help

JAPHET. *(Echo.)* help

SHEM. Mother, we pray you all together
    Come into the ship for fear of the weather.

NOAH'S WIFE. How can we trust our maker anymore?
    My will is just as iron as before!

> (*A furious* **LARKING** *appears as* **GOD** – *an unplanned intervention.*)

GOD. Stubborn wife, whose mouth runneth freely
    I, your *God*, commandeth...theely.
    Halt this madness and board the ark
    Or *all* of us shall drown.
    (All of you, I mean.)

> (**HOLLIS** *delivers the following clear-eyed – on the verge of contemporary, naturalistic acting:*)

NOAH'S WIFE. For the sake of all the luckless others
    For children lost and for their mothers
    For buried friends and buried brothers
    For those already gone to ill,
    I now submit unto Thy will.

> (*At last she boards the ark.*)

SHEM. Welcome

HAM. Welcome

JAPHET. Welcome, Mother, to this boat

NOAH'S WIFE. Now have thou *that* for thy note!

(*She cuffs "**JAPHET**" on the head and his wooden head goes flying off, into the seats.*)

(*From somewhere far off, far above the audience's heads, through an opening in a brick wall, comes a hearty chuckle. The* **DUKE**. *The actors look up. The chuckle goes on and on. They don't know whether or not to continue.*)

Scene Seven

(LARKING, HOLLIS, GREGORY, and the PHYSIC back in their chamber. They all look down at their feet. A long silence, then:)

LARKING. You've condemned us all. You know that?

HOLLIS. I do.

LARKING. You've murdered us all –

PHYSIC. That's / enough

LARKING. *(Continuous.)* And not a word in your defense!

HOLLIS. It felt right, is all.

LARKING. "Felt," always felt. Did you have accomplices? *(He looks at the PHYSIC.)* Him?

HOLLIS. What choice did he have?

LARKING. In front of the fucking Duke.

GREGORY. Shouldn't say fucking Duke.

(The MAJOR-DOMO is suddenly in the doorway.)

MAJOR-DOMO. Well then.

(They all stand as he enters the room. He unrolls a little scroll.)

A message from his excellency, the Duke of Travo.

GREGORY. Does that mean he liked it?

(The MAJOR-DOMO ignores this and reads.)

MAJOR-DOMO. "Players all,

First, let me congratulate you on a most comic and diverting evening" –

LARKING. "Comic," what's he mean, comic?

HOLLIS. Shhh.

MAJOR-DOMO. "Your 'God' was an enjoyably pompous buffoon, amusingly in love with the sound of his own voice. *(LARKING silently fumes.)* More wonderful still were the fisticuffs between poor Noah and his saucy spouse. As a married man, I can well appreciate the trials of a disobedient wife.

Now with thanks I send you on your way –

And because you have pleased me so well, a new honor: You may now call yourselves The Duke of Travo Players. We look forward to your return next Christmastime."

(He looks up from the page.)

Well. I think you've made rather a hit with the Duke.

*(**LARKING** looks at his feet. A gathering storm.)*

LARKING. Send us on our way?

MAJOR-DOMO. I can't remember hearing kinder words from His Highness.

LARKING. That's it? Thank you and goodbye and have a nice life? Or a nice death, / more like?

PHYSIC. Larking, steady / now –

LARKING. No – not Larking, steady! Don't you understand, we'll die out there!

MAJOR-DOMO. This is not a refuge, it's a working village. Only those with a real purpose in society earn their shelter.

LARKING. Purpose, did you hear that? We don't serve a purpose!

MAJOR-DOMO. *(Helpfully.)* Like a butler or a horseman

LARKING. I thought – I told all these souls –

HOLLIS. It will be all right

LARKING. Will it?

PHYSIC. We'll keep moving, we'll outrun the sickness. It's worked so far.

LARKING. Did it work for Brom? Or Henry?

HOLLIS. You're the man who said don't just lie down and die.

"The Duke of Travo Players." *(Not entirely believing this, perhaps.)* We'll say that name and doors will open for us. Doors that were shut before.

(Beat.)

LARKING. *(To himself, desolate.)* I thought this was the ark.

HOLLIS. What?

LARKING. I thought this was the ark. But there isn't any ark.

Scene Eight

(RONA sits up in her cot. She looks very weak, but she's turned a corner. The cards are spread before her.)

RONA. St. Felicitas, I asked you for a son

Not a lemon-faced girl.

St. Felicitas, you don't listen

Or you don't care

Or you don't fucking exist.

(She swipes the cards off the bed.)

Now I've got nothing but me

And that's not much.

(A knock on the door.)

What.

(GREGORY enters.)

But the quarantine – they say I'm poison for another week.

GREGORY. You're not poison.

RONA. No more than usual.

GREGORY. *("You don't understand.")* I prayed for you and it bled. *(He takes the nail out of his pocket.)* The Christ-nail bled, like he said it would.

(She just looks at him. Then she starts to pick up the cards. GREGORY moves to help.)

RONA. Don't. There's an order.

(In another part of the stage, HOLLIS and the PHYSIC:)

PHYSIC. You kissed me.

HOLLIS. *(Playfully obtuse.)* Did I?

PHYSIC. I wasn't sure if it was just

HOLLIS. A fluke?

PHYSIC. Or for the play.

HOLLIS. I don't think Noah's Wife is much of a kisser.

PHYSIC. No

HOLLIS. Efficient at procreation, maybe.

PHYSIC. They had to be doing *some*thing for forty days.

HOLLIS. *(A beat.)* "Asher."

PHYSIC. What

HOLLIS. Just seeing how it sounds – I never get to say it.

PHYSIC. You kept my secret.

HOLLIS. Before we even met, someone warned me about you.

PHYSIC. But something changed your mind.

HOLLIS. I think… I stopped believing in that kind of magic.

PHYSIC. *(Dismissive.)* Ghosts. Spells.

We are more alone in the world than we thought.

> *(Just then,* **RONA** *finishes picking up the tarot cards. For a moment the scenes intersect:)*

GREGORY. I think about that night, all the time. The night you came to me.

RONA. *("You think a lot of yourself.")* Oh, I came to you, did I?

HOLLIS. Are we?

PHYSIC. ?

HOLLIS. Alone?

GREGORY. Yes.

RONA. I think about it too.

GREGORY. You do?

RONA. Don't make me say it again.

HOLLIS. What if, when we forget magic, we make room for something else?

> *(***GREGORY** *kisses* **RONA,** *lightly.)*

> *(During the following, the* **PHYSIC** *takes* **HOLLIS***'s hand in his.)*

GREGORY. Soon as the quarantine is up, we're moving on.

RONA. Where?

GREGORY. The next city, the next square. Mr. Larking says I can play Shem now. So you don't have to be both. You can just be a lady.

RONA. A lady, is that what I am.

GREGORY. Yes. *(Beat.)* Do you think you might come to me again, sometime?

RONA. Who can say?

(A feeling that she definitely will.)

Life is long.

(She looks out the window at the coming spring.)

Scene Nine

> *(Time has passed.* **NOAH** *and* **NOAH'S WIFE**
> *watch the flood waters retreating. A miniature*
> *Ark is perched atop a forced-perspective*
> *Mount Ararat.* **RONA** *and* **GREGORY** *look*
> *on from the flies, operating the pulleys and*
> *ropes together.)*

NOAH. Now all the sorrows we were in,
    And all our trials, are no more.

NOAH'S WIFE. But Noah, where are all our kin
    And company we knew before?

NOAH. All are drowned – spare me your din –
    For all their sins they paid, full sore.
    A better life let us begin,
    So that we grieve our God no more.

NOAH'S WIFE. But husband, how shall our lives be led,
    Since none are in this world but we?

NOAH. Our children shall each other wed
    And thus shall multiply their seed!

> *(Maybe* **NOAH'S WIFE** *finds this a little*
> *questionable.)*

They'll till the soil and bake the bread
And soon, a world shall begin to be.

> *(In the wings, the* **PLAYWRIGHT** *seems agitated.*
> *From across the stage, he locks eyes with the*
> *actor who plays* **HOLLIS**.*)*

> *(As they talk,* Noah's Flood *continues, mutely.*
> **NOAH** *raises the olive branch to the heavens*
> *in thanks to* **GOD**).)*

PLAYWRIGHT. What are you thinking, at the end?

HOLLIS. *(A beat.)* I'm not gonna lie, sometimes I'm thinking
    about dinner. Or "*[Name of actor]*, do your laundry."
    And then I feel guilty, because everyone in the world
    just died and I'm thinking about dinner. But – she
    must've had that moment too.

PLAYWRIGHT. Noah's Wife.

> *(From the wings, **RONA** turns a crank and the floodwaters recede.)*

HOLLIS. And Hollis. At some point you have to think about dinner. The persistence of the normal is strong. And I guess it's sad that we forget so easily, that the people of the future will never understand –

PLAYWRIGHT. But maybe that's how we're able to move forward.

HOLLIS. People have always thought the world was about to end. They've been saying it for a thousand years. And yet –

PLAYWRIGHT. *(Facile.)* Here we are.

HOLLIS. Something's wrong. What's wrong?

> *(Behind them, **NOAH** looks skyward as **GOD** descends from on high. **LARKING** starts to deliver a long and decorous speech that we can't hear. The **PLAYWRIGHT** takes in the play happening around them:)*

PLAYWRIGHT. I just don't know if we deserve it.

> *(A confused beat.)*

HOLLIS. Deserve what?

PLAYWRIGHT. The happy ending.

HOLLIS. Oh

PLAYWRIGHT. We all know how *Noah's Flood* ends. The water recedes and the sun shines, and rainbows –

HOLLIS. What's wrong with that?

PLAYWRIGHT. It says the crisis is over, and I guess that's not the way I feel. It's more like...

HOLLIS. *("I know what you mean.")* The sky is still falling.

RONA. *(From the wings, a stage whisper.)* Gregory!

PLAYWRIGHT. I'm worried we're saying the work is done, just by ending the play. When it's just starting.

> *(In the wings, **RONA** struggles with the heavy rope that's meant to pull the storm clouds offstage.)*

RONA. Gregory, I need you!

HOLLIS. Uh, I think she's trying to –

PLAYWRIGHT. *(Ignoring* **RONA**.*)* That's the trouble with catharsis, it's innately complacent.

> *(***RONA*** *comes on stage and physically drags him back into the wings.)*

HOLLIS. But it's so delicious.

> *(He and* **RONA** *pull the ropes, and the dark clouds track off. Divine sunlight rains down on us. Catharsis.)*

PLAYWRIGHT. And then, what's the opposite of catharsis?

> *(Before she can answer, focus shifts back to Noah's Ark:)*

GOD. Noah, take thy wife anon,
And thy children – every one.
From the ship thou shalt be gone,
And to a world more free.

> *(***NOAH*** *and* **NOAH'S WIFE** *exit the ark and enter the bright new world, arm in arm.)*

GOD. Beasts and all that cannest fly
Out anon with you shall they
On earth to grow and multiply;
I will that it so be.
Grow, and multiply, and *live* –
I will that it so be.

> *(***GOD*** *looks out at us in the audience.)*

My blessing now I give thee here:
From now no longer need you fear
My storm clouds shall no more appear;
And now farewell, my darlings dear.

End of Play

AUTHOR'S NOTE

In early workshops of the play, Heidi Schreck played the role of Hollis. I commissioned Heidi to write a monologue from the actor's perspective to enhance Act II, and she responded with the wonderful account of her experience playing Mrs. Cratchit at Actors Theatre of Louisville. Because it isn't realistic for Heidi to always play herself when *The Amateurs* is presented, we devised a solution where the role is named for whichever actress is playing Hollis at the moment. So, in the Vineyard Theatre production, Quincy Tyler Bernstine delivers the Mrs. Cratchit monologue as if the words are her own. If it's possible to preserve this illusion for audiences, we'd greatly appreciate it. Thank you!

Lightning Source UK Ltd.
Milton Keynes UK
UKHW021950220920
370355UK00006B/266

9 780573 707841